BUTTERFLY BEACH

Words and pictures by Polly Caldwell Bookwalter

MONTECITO SHORES PUBLISHING

For Beth and Brian

Order: Lepidoptera
Latin name: *Danaus plexippus*
Common name: Monarch

Over one million Monarch butterflies migrate southward along the west coast of the United States each year. There are more than 200 Monarch over-wintering sites along the California coast. Many of these sites are threatened by development, the loss of trees, and changes to the Monarch's unique habitat that is vital to their survival.

This book belongs to

Nestled between purple mountains
and a glistening turquoise sea in southern
California is a pretty little beach.

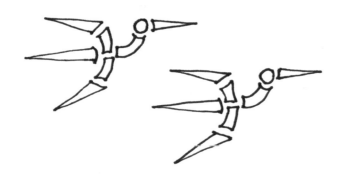
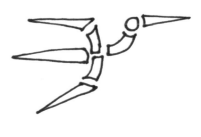

Snowy white pelicans glide majestically in the bright blue sky.

Funny birds with short legs and long beaks skitter
about chasing the waves.

Shiny gray dolphins swim in the salty water.

Seals rest on the warm sandy shore.

Every night, like magic, the big orange
sun sinks into the horizon...the sky
turns an electric shade of pink...the sea
shimmers with silver...and the rocky
cliffs are flushed with gold.

Every day is the same,
except in the winter when...

...the butterflies arrive!

For many years, millions of butterflies filled the sky with their bright orange wings.

They came from thousands of miles away to escape the cold weather in the north.

The little beach was a perfect winter home.

The butterflies frolicked in the grove of big leafy eucalyptus trees near the water's edge.

They flitted and fluttered amongst the clusters of flowers on the hillside, drinking sweet nectar.

They made friends with the dolphins
jumping and splashing in the ocean waves.

They visited the seals sitting on the sand
soaking up the sunshine.

They chased the funny birds with short legs
and long beaks scurrying about on the beach.

When the stars came out and the moon glowed in the
darkness, the butterflies sheltered in the thick grove
of eucalyptus trees.

They clustered close together on the trunks and branches
to stay warm and be protected from the cool ocean breeze.

They rested, listening to the gentle lapping of the waves…
waiting for another day to begin.

When spring arrived, the butterflies said
good-bye to their seaside friends and flew
back to their home in the north...

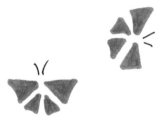

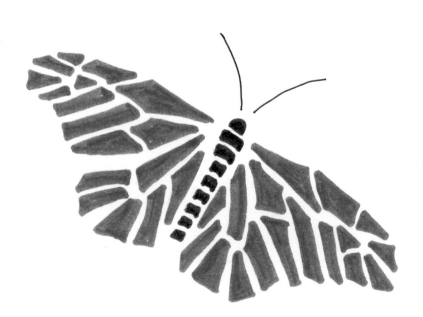

but they never forgot the pretty little beach.

One winter followed another, and as one year turned
into the next, the butterflies came to the pretty
little beach to bask in the warm California sunshine...
to drink the sweet nectar of the flowers on the
hillside…and to sleep in the eucalyptus groves.

Then, one year...

...something changed.

In the daytime, there were strange new noises.

Children were laughing and playing ball on the sand...and swimming and surfing in the water.

People were walking dogs and sitting in chairs under beach umbrellas.

The butterflies were surprised and curious and
flew down to the beach to investigate.

People pointed at the butterflies and smiled.

The children giggled and squealed and
chased the butterflies.

It wasn't long before the butterflies
heard people calling the little beach…

Butterfly Beach.

Each year, Butterfly Beach became busier.
Before long, a wall and steps were built
to make it easier to get to the water.
Trees were cut down to make room
for houses and roads. And people came
in their cars with beach umbrellas and
chairs and sand toys and surfboards.

They swam and frolicked in the rolling
waves, basked in the warm sunshine, and
listened to the crashing surf.

They watched the sun rise in the morning and
set in the evening…and they came to see the
butterflies at Butterfly Beach.

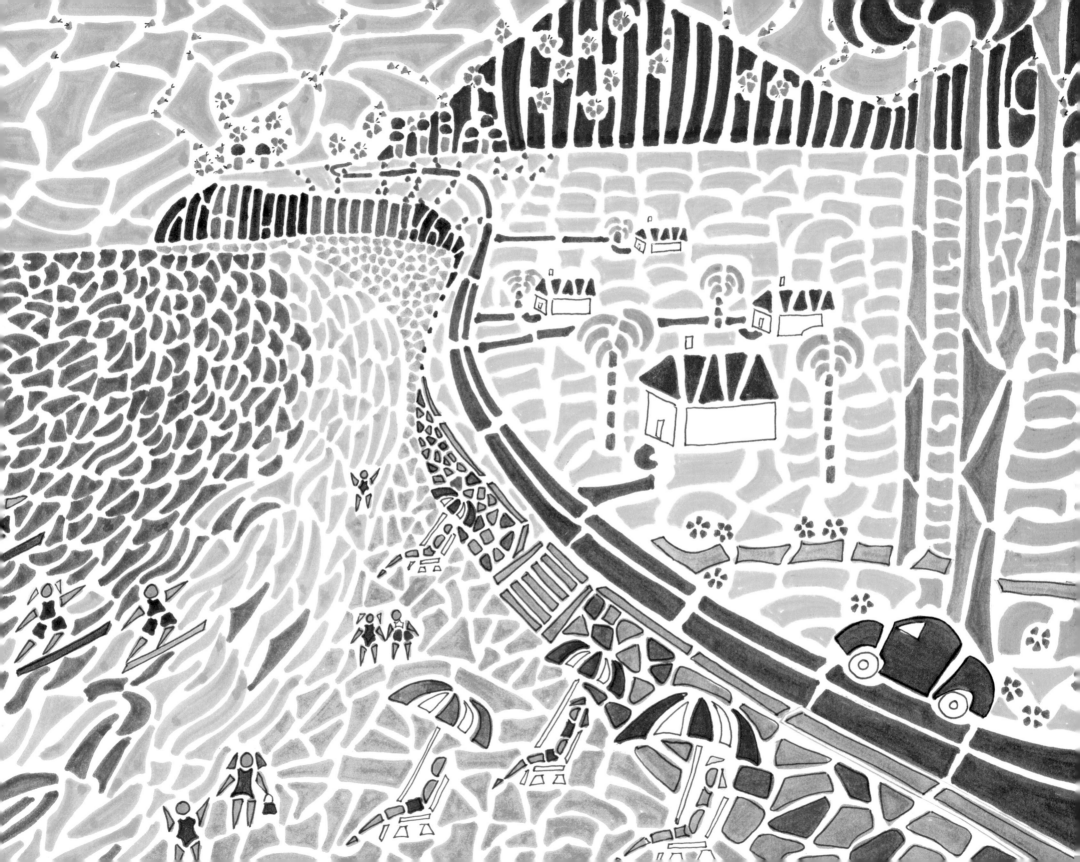

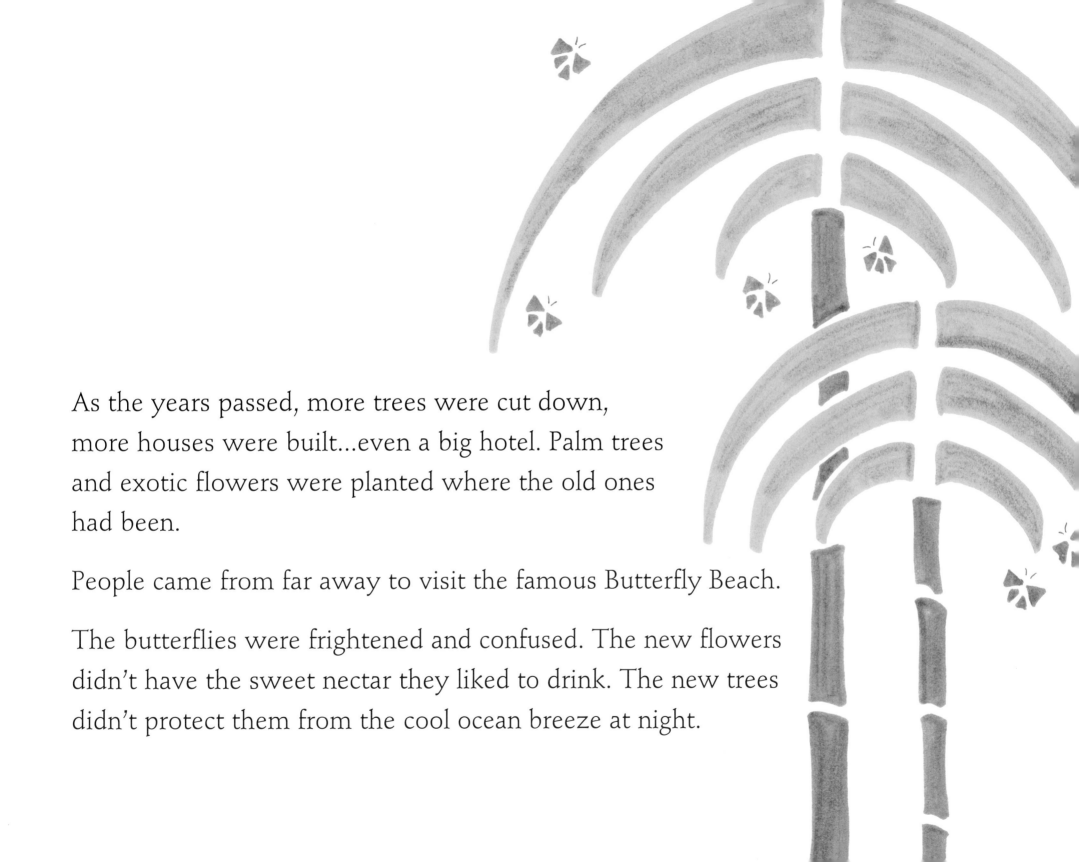

As the years passed, more trees were cut down, more houses were built...even a big hotel. Palm trees and exotic flowers were planted where the old ones had been.

People came from far away to visit the famous Butterfly Beach.

The butterflies were frightened and confused. The new flowers didn't have the sweet nectar they liked to drink. The new trees didn't protect them from the cool ocean breeze at night.

When the butterflies left that spring, they knew they could not come back to the pretty little beach.

They would have to find another place to spend the winter.

People still came to Butterfly Beach…with beach umbrellas and chairs and sand toys and surfboards.

They came to swim and frolic in the rolling waves, to walk their dogs on the sand, to bask in the warm sunshine, and to listen to the crashing surf.

They came to watch the sun rise in the morning and set in the evening…

    …and they came to see the butterflies.

But…

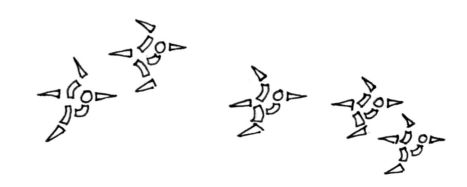

…there were **no butterflies**.

There were no butterflies on the sand…or on the cliffs.

There were no butterflies in the daytime…or at night.

There were no more butterflies at Butterfly Beach…not even one!

The people were sad. The children cried.

Then, after being sad for a long time, the people decided to do something. If they had made the butterflies go away, why couldn't they bring the butterflies back?

They remembered that when the sun was big and warm in the sky, the butterflies used to flitter and flutter about, drinking the sweet nectar of the flowers on the hillside.

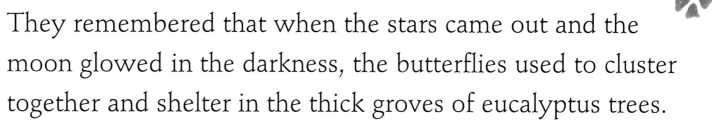

They remembered that when the stars came out and the moon glowed in the darkness, the butterflies used to cluster together and shelter in the thick groves of eucalyptus trees.

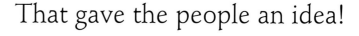

That gave the people an idea!

If they replanted the kinds of flowers and trees the butterflies liked…maybe the butterflies would come back.

So they got started planting eucalyptus trees. People who lived near the pretty little beach made room in their yards for more flowers…and the hotel even made a butterfly garden.

Today, the butterflies are beginning to return to Butterfly Beach. More and more come back each winter. It is the happiest time of the year.

People come to the pretty little beach to swim and walk and play, to fish and surf, to paint and read, to strum guitars and sing.

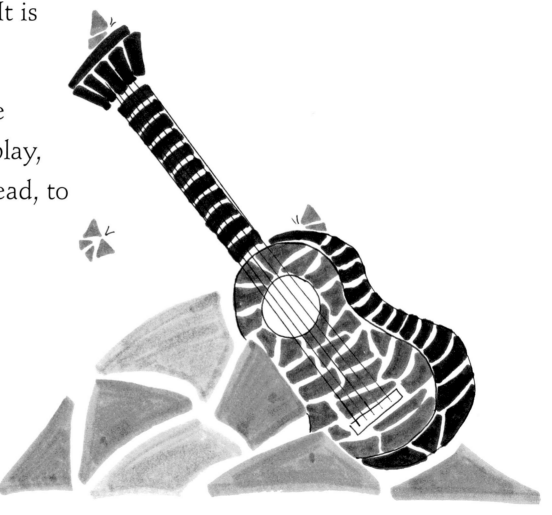

They even come to Butterfly Beach
to be married on the sand.

They look out at the glistening turquoise sea.

They watch the sun rise in the morning
and set in the evening,
and they look for the butterflies,

and...

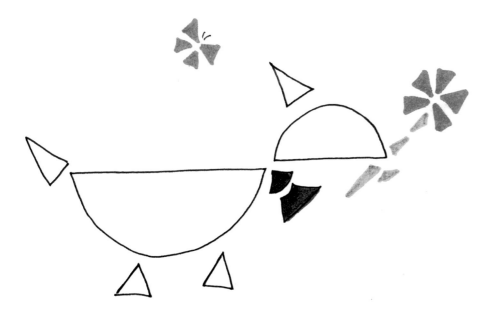

…the butterflies are there!

They make the people point and smile. They make the children giggle and squeal.

They flap their wings and glide through the bright blue sky over the pretty little beach.

They flitter and flutter amongst the clusters of flowers on the hillside, drinking sweet nectar.

They visit the dolphins and the seals and the funny birds with short legs and long beaks, and they sleep in the cozy eucalyptus trees at night…resting, listening to the gentle lapping of the waves on the sand…

…waiting for another day to begin.

The end.

Published by Montecito Shores Publishing
44 Seaview Drive, Santa Barbara, CA 93108, USA
Website: www.butterflybeachonline.com

Design/Production by Margaret Dodd, Studio K Communication Arts
Printed in China

ISBN 978-0-9793280-0-8

Publisher's Cataloging-in-Publication
(Provided by Quality Books, Inc.)

Bookwalter, Polly Caldwell.
    Butterfly beach / written and illustrated by Polly Caldwell Bookwalter.
    p. cm.
    SUMMARY: Describes the impact of beach development on the migratory patterns of monarch butterflies along the California coast. When butterflies stop wintering at Butterfly Beach, local residents bring them back by recreating the lost environment that these butterflies need.
    Audience: Ages 1-8.
    LCCN 2007922426
    ISBN-13: 978-0-9793280-0-8
    ISBN-10: 0-9793280-0-4
    1. Monarch butterfly--Juvenile fiction. 2. Monarch butterfly--Migration--California—Juvenile fiction. 3. Monarch butterfly--Conservation--California—Juvenile fiction. [1. Monarch butterfly--Fiction. 2. Butterflies--Fiction. 3. Wildlife conservation--Fiction.] I. Title.
PZ7.B64575But 2007   [E]
                QBI07-600068